CHAPTER ONE

Space travel sucks sometimes.

The thought crossed through Carlton's mind as, for the three-hundredth time this shift, he checked the navigation display. Just as it almost always did, the ship's position tracked exactly with projections.

Terribly boring.

But then, that was to be expected of interstellar travel. With hundreds of thousands of Astronomical Units—AUs—to cover, even a relatively short trip could take years. Unfortunately, this was no short trip. The run from the Gliese system to Earth, though routine, was also 20.5 light years in length. Even at the ship's cruising speed of 95% of the speed of light (.95c), it would take almost six and a half years to complete the trip. Of course, it took a little less than a year to get up to cruising speed, and another year to slow back down again, so the total trip was closer to ten years. But it could be worse. Without the time dilation caused by relativity, it would be almost twenty-five years.

God bless Einstein.

It was just rotten luck that Carlton drew this portion of

the trip. The center passage was mind numbingly dull: nothing much to do for the year but monitor instruments and readouts and maybe make a slight course correction every now and then. Which is why it paid the least. But everyone drew the short stick sometimes.

He tapped the upper right corner of the display, and it shifted from Navigation to Engineering. Another tap pulled up the reactor specs.

Located two kilometers aft of the crewed area of the ship to save on shielding material, the reactor was an old-style fission device. Newer ships had fusion generators these days, of course. But construction on Pericles completed two years before Kilpatrick and Holbert patented the containment device that made fusion practical, and there was no point in scrapping a new and perfectly capable ship just because some new tech came along.

So the Company put Pericles in service on the Gliese run. This was her fourth transit of the interstellar void. When they reached earth, it would be time for her hundred-year overhaul.

That didn't make a whole lot of sense to Carlton. Sure, Pericles would be about a hundred Earth years old when they docked, but she had only experienced a little less than 40 years of time-dilated service. No one asked him, though. He was just the driver.

The reactor specs all fell in the normal range. No surprise there, considering that without the plasma generators online to power the main engines, the reactor put out just a small fraction of its rated power.

Carlton moved on to life support.

Again, everything read normal. Consumables were depleting as expected. The crops in the hydroponics section were looking good, and the waste reclamation system was churning along nicely. Carlton expected this, as the system was operating at much less than its maximum capacity.

Next, gravity.

The crewed section of the ship consisted of two rings, each a kilometer in diameter and fifty meters wide, with three decks. They connected to the central hub of the ship through four passage tubes, and rotated continually in opposite directions during cruise flight to simulate gravity. During acceleration to and deceleration from cruise speed, the main engines provided all the G forces necessary.

Though initially set to simulate Gliese-normal gravity, the computer system slowly lowered the rotation period so that, at the end of the journey, gravity would be reduced to Earth-normal. The slow transition made it easy for the crew and passengers to acclimate to their new environs before arrival. That was one good thing about these longer passages. The passage from the Centauri colony was short enough for the transition to be difficult for some people. None of that trouble on the Gliese run, though.

Accelerometers in each section of A and B rings sent readouts to the display monitor. 10.36 m/sec2. Right on track.

Carlton pulled up cryogenics.

Cryo was the most important system on the ship, at least to the eggheads at Corporate. Five thousand passengers, plus the rest of the crew aside from Carlton's shift, peacefully slept away the cruise under cryo-suspension, with periodically programmed massage and movement sessions. Cryo-suspension did not completely stop metabolic processes, after all. The nearly ten year passage would be equivalent to about six months of normal aging: long enough for the passengers to suffer severe muscle atrophy if they were not kept in motion periodically. They, and the cargo in the holds, were the reason Carlton was here. Their fares paid his commission, so he supposed cryo was the most important system for him, too.

He chuckled at that thought.

Just one last thing to check. Carlton punched up the external sensors and began a scan.

First, the hull monitoring cameras. Again as usual, he found no blemishes on the hull.

Next, the forward looking scanners. Pericles had radar units, of course, but at her current speed, by the time they received the returns, they would be almost on any objects in their path. And while starliners were equipped with exterior coils that generated a magnetic field to repel charged particles, the field did nothing for solid objects. Even a tiny object could create a fatal collision at relativistic speeds. The destruction of the Avalon, one of the first transport vessels to the Gliese system, was reportedly caused by a collision with a meteor the size of a melon.

To help defend against that, and to assist with navigation, the Company deployed and maintained a quartet of beacons every few light-hours along the spacelanes between the various colonies. Every starliner carried a few beacons to replace units that were approaching end of life or whose orbit had carried them too far from the most efficient course between stars. Pericles had just three days earlier deployed four to replace an aging quartet. The beacons transmitted coded radio signals. Pericles carried receiver units tuned for them, and could use the signals to help triangulate her position as well as detect objects ahead by interpolating the interference patterns between the signals from the beacons. It was a pretty efficient system, all things considered.

It took just a second to update the ahead display after Carlton shifted over from the cameras. There were no objects of concern within the next four hours of travel. Satisfied, Carlton set the automatic monitoring system to issue an alert if it detected anything, then pushed back from his console.

The bridge was smaller than a lay person might expect for

a ship Pericles' size: just a pilot station, a communications panel, and a command console for the Captain, all situated in a small bubble atop the hull, with viewing windows in all directions. The Captain's station was astern and above the others. All were nestled between stairs leading back to the aft bulkhead, where the hatch to the rest of the ship nestled in the floor. During acceleration, crewmembers could walk up the stairs to sit in the chairs, their backs to the G forces.

Carlton could have run the diagnostic programs from a workstation in the command center down in the crew quarters, but he rather enjoyed coming up here. For one thing, it had some of the only windows on the ship without a rotating view. It was nice to be able to look at one point in space without losing it after a few seconds.

Of course, the view at cruising speed was different, disconcerting to the un-initiated. The light from the stars ahead was so blueshifted that very little was actually visible to the eye. The stars astern were redshifted similarly. But looking athwartships one could almost think one was looking up at a normal night sky from the surface of a planet somewhere.

Almost.

The other thing he enjoyed was being in zero-G. No matter how many times he experienced it, Carlton never quite got over how different, and fun, it was. Some people got space sick from being in zero-G for too long, but he never had. He almost wished he could spend the whole trip like this. But he wasn't a big fan of losing all muscle tone and getting brittle bones, so he did not wish too hard.

Carlton only lingered for a moment before pushing himself through the hatch to the central corridor of the hub.

Handholds on the walls made for easy travel through the bulkheads and hatches that separated the bridge from the crew's acceleration quarters, and then through more bulkheads to the junction with Ring A, two hundred meters aft. During acceleration, the handholds would be ladder rungs, and the corridor a vertical shaft between decks. Yes, it was much more fun moving around during cruise, in zero-G.

At the junction, he took a moment to locate the tunnel to section four. It was always a bit annoying getting into the lift, with the hatch rotating around the junction, but he managed it without too much trouble.

The hatch slid shut behind him, and Carlton found himself pressed up against one wall as the ring's rotation met his body and carried it along. Positioning himself feet "down", toward the ring itself, he pushed himself to what would be the lift's floor once the G's began to build up and pushed the button for the first deck.

Ring A, Section Four, First Deck was crew quarters. The rest of Ring A contained consumables storage, hydroponics, life support equipment, and passenger berthing. Ring B was completely taken up with cargo storage. As with buildings planetside, the rings' decks were numbered from bottom to top, so the first deck was the outermost and the third deck the innermost on the ring.

It took two and a half minutes to descend the five hundred meters to the first deck. By then, Carlton's feet were planted firmly on the floor, and he felt normal gravity, or at least a close approximation. If he threw a ball, it would not fly exactly the same way it would in a real gravity well, but it was close enough to do the job.

The lift door opened, and he stepped out into a small alcove, recessed in the aft wall of the main corridor. The wall directly opposite the lift door was terraced, almost like stairs turned on their sides.

Stepping into the corridor itself, Carlton noted as usual how it curved upward noticeably in each direction. The corridor was tiled in light brown tiles that, barring close inspection, were easy to mistake for wood. Faux-wood panels on the walls and softly glowing light fixtures at regular intervals combined with potted plants every so often gave the passage a somewhat homey feel. Prints of various artwork hung on the walls as well, except on the lift side of the corridor, to the left. During acceleration, the changing crew shifts could walk up the stairs in the wall from the lift, then down the corridor to the crew's cryo-suspension beds.

Newcomers to space travel might be surprised at the decor, very much like a nice hotel, but researchers long ago discovered that the more comfortable people were in their living quarters, the less stressful they found long duration space flight. For the passengers, this was not a concern. They entered cryo-suspension not long after boarding, before the ship actually got underway, and awoke after the ship moored. But the crew had to live aboard, so starliner designers tried to make their living arrangements as close to luxury as they could.

Carlton found the Duty Captain in the command center, fifty meters down the corridor to the right. She was sitting at her desk near the back of the room, dressed in the light grey coveralls that all starliner crewmembers wore underway and sipping on a cup of coffee as she watched the news feed on a view screen.

The news came across on the coded signal from the beacons. While it was very time late, it helped morale to have some notion of what was going on at their destination. It beat showing up to the planet and having no idea of recent history on the ground.

Seeing her alone, Carlton grunted. "Where is everyone?"

The Captain shrugged. "Bryce went off to fix a problem in the galley. Malcolm and Stephanie are helping teach science class."

Bryce was one of the two general technicians on the shift.

Malcolm was the shift engineer, and Stephanie one of the reactor techs.

Each shift manned the ship for one year of the passage, and was kept as small as possible. In general, a shift consisted of the Duty Captain, two pilots, the shift engineer, two reactor techs, the doctor, two cooks, two horticulturists, two general techs, and the teacher. Plus the crew's children. The pilots, techs, and cooks swapped twelve hour watches. The others were on call as needed, but generally worked a normal day.

"Ah. Well everything looks good. Right on the money." Carlton walked over to her desk to get a better look at the view screen. "Anything interesting going on?"

"More riots in Brazil. Looks like it's getting pretty bad."

"Well, it's nothing we need to worry about. If you need me, I'll be helping Alison."

"Right."

It became very obvious, in the earliest of humanity's excursions to the stars over five hundred years ago, that it was asking far too much for a person to leave family behind while embarking on a decades-long journey. By the time a starfarer returned from even a short trip, he would have missed much of his kids' childhood, to say nothing of the toll it took on marriages.

So almost from the beginning, crewmembers brought their families with them. Large as the starliners were, though, extraneous personnel were a burden, so family members learned tasks to assist in running the ships. Case in point, Alison was Carlton's wife, and the shift's doctor.

Eventually, the crews of the various ships became more extended families than colleagues, and the starfarers developed a culture altogether unique from the ground-based. Entire generations were born, lived, and died working on the starliners. Sure, some crewmembers left after their initial contracts expired, deciding they preferred life planetside. And some children opted for a different life as well. But for the most part, starfarers were a distinct clan.

Like him, Alison was raised on a starliner. They met on shore leave five years ago. When it came time for her to ship out again, he arranged a transfer onto Pericles to be with her. The rest, as they say, was history.

Carlton found her in the clinic, taking an inventory of the various drugs in storage. Managing medical supplies was tricky on long voyages. Drug expiration had to be carefully tracked, and fresh supplies removed from cryo-freeze early to avoid any gaps in availability during the long thawing process. Carlton did not envy her that.

Alison looked up as Carlton entered and beamed at him. "A letter from Sasha came over a few minutes ago. He got into Harvard Med!"

Sasha was her younger brother, stationed on another starliner on the Gliese route. Family members who were not on the same ship almost always worked to remain on the same route. It often worked out that they were able to see each other on shore leave on one side of the route or other. With the time compression of cryo-suspension, that generally worked out to seeing each other every three or four waking years, for a few months at a time.

Carlton returned Alison's smile. "That's great! When does he start school?"

"They're four earth-years ahead of us on the route, so he should be just about finishing when we arrive."

"Just in time for graduation. That should be a good party."

Alison nodded. "And we're rolling to shore duty, so we can be there for his residency."

Shore duty. It was both cherished and dreaded.

Starfarers got leave at the end of each run while maintenance crews worked on the ship. Depending on how much was planned for the upkeep, they could get anywhere from three to six months off. But this run was different. Pericles' overhaul was scheduled to take almost four years. That was too long for the crew to do nothing, so typically they were assigned to train new hires or manage projects at the corporate headquarters. It was good, in a sense. Being in one place for a while had its advantages.

But a body could grow soft, too. Especially for people with children in their teen years, being ashore that long carried its own worries. Most children who opted out of the starfarers' life were teenagers planetside on shore duty. They lost their love for the ships during that time and left, leaving their parents with an impossible choice: to leave the lives they loved or the kids they loved.

That's why most of the short-hop starliners were manned with older crews. The crewmembers could continue their jobs, but still see their kids every few earth years. It was a compromise many made that seemed to work out. Fortunately for Carlton and Alison, their son was only three, so that worry was a long way off, still.

Carlton was about to respond when the first few bars from Beethoven's Fifth Symphony emanated from the console on the wall and drew his attention. Each crewmember wore locator devices that allowed the ship's internal sensors to keep track of them and forward calls wherever they were onboard. Beethoven's Fifth was Carlton's "ring tone", to borrow a phrase from ancient Earth history.

He walked over to the console and tapped the screen. An automated message popped up. Forward sensors had detected something ahead.

Carlton frowned in annoyance. Probably just another rogue asteroid crossing their path. All the same, he had to check it out.

"I gotta go back to the bridge, babe. Be back in a bit."

Five minutes later, he floated up to his pilot's console and woke it up with a tap on the screen. A couple taps later he had the forward sensors called up.

This was no asteroid.

Whatever it was, it was big, about a light-hour ahead, and traveling on a near-collision course with them. The doppler readout indicated the object was traveling at .8c: slower than a starliner, but definitely not natural.

Carlton punched up the intercom to the command center.

"Yeah Carl. What's up?"

"Better get up here, Cap'n."

In the few minutes it took the Captain to get to the bridge, Carlton entered the commands to wake up the lower forward observation camera. Essentially a 4 meter telescope mounted beneath the bow of the ship, the camera, and its fellows mounted just aft of the bridge and above and below the main engines' fuel tanks aft, was onboard for just this purpose.

The camera finished warming up and was beginning to zoom in on the approaching object when the Captain arrived at his side.

"Object ahead, Cap'n. Moving too fast to be an asteroid."

Her eyes scanned the sensor readout quickly, and she nodded agreement.

"Another starliner?"

"Not supposed to be another until Haverly, next month. Besides, this thing's too slow."

"Maybe..."

The Captain's words stuck in her throat as the image from the camera filled the screen.

It was difficult to make out in the faint illumination from the distant stars, but it was definitely a vessel. It was of no design Carlton had ever seen, though, and he had seen them all. No rings, no plasma engine nacelles. It was crescent-shaped, off-white in color, and tumbled slowly end over end through space.

"What the hell is that?" Carlton breathed.

The Captain was silent for a long minute, her expression one of curiosity.

"What's the CPA?"

"Wait one." Carlton tapped the display, and the data came up. "Closest Point of Approach: .75 AU, Bearing 328 mark 47, in one hour, seven minutes." A CPA above Pericles and to the left explained why he did not detect the vessel earlier. Though it was in their plane of travel now, it must have drifted up from below.

"Hmm. On that trajectory, it didn't come from Earth. Any other colonies out that way?"

Carlton shook his head. Even before calling up the nav display, he knew the answer.

"Closest is Talos, but that thing's forty degrees off course to have come from there."

There was a long silence as they watched the strange ship grow slowly larger on the camera display. Carlton knew the Captain was thinking the same thing as he, but it was too incredible to voice.

"Maybe whatever crippled it knocked it off course."

The Captain snorted.

"What do we do?"

Pushing herself away from the pilot's console, the Captain floated to the starboard side viewing window. She looked out at the passing stars for a while.

Carlton alternated between watching her and the approaching ship. He knew better than to press too hard, though. When she got pensive like this, the Captain could be snippy.

Eventually, she spoke, in the tone she used when she really meant business.

"Keep watching it, and let me know if anything changes. Be sure to record everything. I'm going below to check on a couple things, but I'll be back before it reaches CPA."

With that, she pushed off and floated back to the entrance hatch. Before she disappeared below, she issued a final order.

"Keep this quiet, Carl. Lock out the workstations in the ring, and don't breathe a word to anyone until I get back."

Carlton blinked. Lock out the workstations? That was almost unheard of. What was she worried about? This was potentially huge! Everyone would want to know. Would *deserve* to know. But he had flown with the Captain for a lot of years, and had learned to trust her judgment.

Obediently, he keyed the commands to restrict access.

CHAPTER TWO

For the next forty-five minutes, Carlton watched the strange ship draw nearer.

As it grew in the display, he made out more details. Strange markings, letters of some kind he thought, but in no language he had ever seen, decorated the hull in a number of places. The hull was breached. Twin cuts, perfectly parallel and framed with dark scorch marks, tore across the vessel's port side. Gasses of some variety or other vented to space through the cuts, slowly increasing the ship's rate of rotation. Whatever happened to that ship, it had occurred recently.

True to her word, the Captain returned to the bridge. As she floated up to the pilot's console, Carlton noticed she had a spiral-bound stack of paper tucked under her arm. Paper! Carlton hadn't seen a paper document since...well, come to think of it, he had *never* seen a paper document. He had heard of people who kept paper books in libraries, collectors and the like. But he did not have that kind of money. Nor did anyone he knew.

"Any change, Carl?"

"Nope. But take a look at this."

Carlton tapped the screen, pausing the image as the twin cuts on the vessel's hull rotated into view.

"Those look like plasma burns to me."

The Captain pursed her lips, nodding in agreement. She leaned forward a bit, peering intently at the image on the screen. As she did, the papers under her arm shifted a bit, and Carlton saw "TOP SECRET: CAPTAIN'S EYES ONLY" written at the top of the title page.

"What's so secret, Cap'n?"

She pulled back, covering the pages up with her free hand for a heartbeat. Then, seeing the knowing look in Carlton's eyes, she sighed and withdrew the papers from under her arm.

"These are procedures to follow in the event a starliner should encounter evidence of intelligent extraterrestrial life."

Carlton's eyebrow twitched upward, but before he could say a word, the Captain wagged a finger at him.

"You never saw these papers, Carl. Understand? It's both our asses, otherwise."

"Come on, Cap'n. What're they gonna..."

She leaned forward, a fierce light in her eyes.

"I'm not screwing around, Carl. We could both disappear if we mess this up."

She tapped a finger on the bottom of the title page, drawing Carl's eye. His protests died on his lips when he saw the name there. Though officially denied, it was common knowledge that the NSA did just that with inconvenient people. He swallowed, despite the fact that his mouth had just gone dry.

"Alright, so what are we supposed to do?"

"Keep an accurate record of the entire event. Take no provocative actions. Send reports to the government."

"You're kidding."

"Huh?"

"That's all stuff we were going to do anyway."

"Well...yeah."

Carlton threw up his hands.

"What the hell's so Top Secret about that?"

The Captain smirked. "Clearly you've never seen classified documents before. The fact that it deals with ETs is what makes it Top Secret." She leaned forward, eyes narrowing as she examined the tumbling ship. "Can you zoom in any further, make this more clear?" She pointed at a single blister-like bubble on the dorsal area of the ship.

Carlton nodded. He tapped on the image, freezing it in place as the bubble rotated into view again. Then with a two-fingered spreading gesture, he activated the display's zoom feature. The image took a few seconds to stabilize. When it resolved, the bubble was more clearly visible. A lone light shone from the bubble, dimly illuminating the forward area of the hull.

"Son of a bitch. It still has power."

"That changes things," said the Captain as she turned toward the communication console. She tapped the console, rousing it from standby, then flipped open her procedure to a page near the back. She frowned, tapping at her lips with her index finger, as she read.

"What are you doing?"

She began tapping on the console, and a screen Carlton had never seen before opened up.

"There are generic communication protocols programmed in the comms system. Peace, friendship, that sort of thing. Procedure states we try to make contact, if possible."

A loud snort was Carlton's initial reply.

"You can't be serious. We don't know what frequencies they use, and..."

The Captain interrupted.

"So we use every frequency we can transmit on."

"Fine, but you can't really think they'll understand, even *if* they receive it."

The Captain opened her mouth to reply, but he kept on talking.

"And even if they did, it's pointless anyway. We can't exactly do anything to help them."

That much was certain. Pericles carried enough fuel for the initial acceleration, deceleration at the destination star system, and intra-system maneuvering. They could stop to render assistance to the other craft, but doing so would strand them in the interstellar void, making the gesture worse than useless. The Captain knew this as well as he did.

"Understood. Regardless, we're going to follow procedure."

With that, she made one last tap on the communication console, and the antenna status indications lit up across all bands as Pericles began transmitting.

She and Carlton both turned their attention to the camera display. They watched intently for any change in the other vessel. Nothing was forthcoming. The vessel continued tumbling, apparently out of control.

Carlton checked the time. Ten minutes to CPA. The vessel's bearing rate had picked up considerably. Tracking had shifted to the forward upper camera, but very soon it would be unable to maintain track. The vessel was simply moving too fast, and was too close. So he directed the aft upper camera toward the vessel's expected departure bearing, in order to pick up visual tracking after it passed CPA.

Despite his misgivings about the transmission, Carlton felt disappointment at the lack of response. Though mankind had been traveling the stars for centuries, and had discovered several dozen life-supporting worlds, the holy grail of meeting an intelligent, sentient alien race had eluded them. There had never even been a hint that anyone else was out there. After so long, most people gave up on the notion, accepting that humanity was alone, at least in this corner of Galaxy. And now, suddenly, to be confronted with an apparent alien artifact...it was unbelievable. Exciting.

And scary.

On the display screen, the strange vessel slipped off frame.

"Lost track due to CPA effect, Cap'n."

"Very well. How long to regain on the other side?"

Carlton tapped the display, and it shifted to a 3-D relative motion display with the vessel's dead reckoning position plotted out in one minute increments.

"Estimated six minutes."

The Captain moved herself closer to the port side viewing window and looked out and upward toward the other vessel's position. Of course it was too far away to see with the naked eye, but Carlton understood the need to look.

"Carl, how close will that thing pass to Gliese?"

That computation was more difficult, but it only took a minute or so.

"About half a parsec. Hard to do a salvage at that distance, if that's what you're thinking."

"True, but it's worth making the attempt."

She turned away from the window and looked at Carlton, her expression one of wonder.

"Of all the ways to meet. Do you have any idea what the odds are of just randomly bumping into them like this?"

He nodded. To say the odds were astronomical would be an understatement. And ironic.

"Guess we should buy lottery tickets when we get..."

An alert flashed on the screen. He tapped the dialogue

window and the display shifted to the aft upper camera. Carlton was gratified to see the vessel centered in the frame.

"Ok, re-acquired visual track on the aft upper camera. Gain bearing and time match predicted."

The Captain moved back next to Carlton, the better to see the display.

"Is it just me, or did something change?"

Carlton frowned, shaking his head.

"Don't think so. We're looking at a different angle..."

He stopped mid-sentence as suddenly something broke off from the vessel's ventral section. Apparently spherical, the object shot straight away from the vessel for a few seconds, then a purple-blue glow appeared on one side of the object, and it moved to the right until it disappeared off frame.

"What the hell was that?" exclaimed the Captain.

"No idea, Cap'n. Tracking in the forward upper camera."

Carlton split the camera display and directed the idle camera over. It took several moments to gain the smaller object, but finally it appeared in frame. Carlton zoomed in tight to pull out more details.

The object was indeed generally spherical. From its angular size and the mother ship's known range, the computer estimated the object's size: 15 meters in diameter. On the near side, he could see a number of protuberances that held what looked like antennas and other sensors. The glow came from nozzles that were just barely visible on the far side of the object; obviously that was a propulsion system of some sort. A few circular outlines, possibly hatches, graced the surface of the object, as did more of that strange script.

Carlton frowned. "It almost looks like a lifepod."

"Where's it going?" The Captain sounded worried.

For that matter, Carlton was beginning to get a case of nerves, too. They were far away from anything and everything here. There was no place for a lifepod to go...except to the

Pericles. But they were moving too fast for a lifepod to catch up.

Weren't they?

Carlton punched up the tracking subroutine and made a few quick computations. He blinked at the results. That couldn't be right. But doing the computations again yielded the same answer.

He cleared his throat. "Ah. Cap'n, based on its change in bearing rate, that thing's decelerating at over ten thousand Gs. If it keeps on like this after it stops, it'll match our forward velocity in just a few minutes."

The Captain's eyebrows climbed high on her forehead.

"How is that possible? That much force would crush that craft and everyone on it!"

"No lie there, Cap'n, but I've run the numbers twice."

"How long until it reaches us?"

Carlton spread his hands helplessly. "Depends how fast it gets. We've got a couple AUs head start. A few hours, probably."

"Son of a..."

A bright flash from the display screen drew their attention once more. The feed from the aft upper camera was whited out for a second while the computer adjusted the camera's gain. When the frame cleared, all that could be seen of the mothership was a rapidly expanding cloud of fragments and heated gas. The vessel had apparently exploded.

Carlton whistled appreciatively.

"Lucky for them they made it off when they did."

"Unless they blew the ship up on purpose."

"Right. Why would they do that?"

The Captain rolled her eyes. "Think about it, Carl. They're probably more advanced than we are. That's a big advantage. They're not going to want to just hand over their ship, with all its technology, for us, or someone else, to reverse engineer."

It had been generations since mankind last warred with itself. But still the memories of the intrigues between nation-states were vivid, kept alive in school as a lesson to the next generation about the foolishness of tribalism and the need to maintain ties between humanity's colonies as close as possible, considering the distances to be traversed. Some organizations, such as the Society for Creative Anachronism, kept the memories alive for entertainment purposes. And of course, businesses still competed against one another, executing their intrigues, very real despite their non-violent nature, in an attempt to gain a competitive edge. So Carl could understand the Captain's logic. It made perfect sense, when he stopped to think about it.

Carlton closed the aft upper camera display, and the life-pod, if that's what it was, filled the entire screen.

"Won't be able to keep this quiet when that thing comes knocking, Cap'n."

"Don't I know it." The Captain exhaled loudly. "Ask Alison to come up, Carl."

He blinked in surprise.

"Say again?"

"Your wife. Have her come up here. Now."

She was back into her no-nonsense voice again. Carlton keyed the intercom, and a moment later Alison answered.

"You've been up there a while. Everything alright?"

"Yeah. Can you come up?"

She didn't answer for several seconds. When she did, she sounded worried.

"What's wrong, honey?"

"Nothing. Just come up please."

The connection closed, and Carlton and the Captain floated in silence, watching the camera display.

Carlton used the time to compute the lifepod's predicted course, and was not surprised to find it on an intercept trajectory. By the time Alison arrived on the bridge, it had completely stopped its motion away from Pericles and was beginning to accelerate toward them.

"Alright, Carl, what's going... What is THAT?"

Alison floated up next to him and the Captain, her jaw hanging open as she looked at the lifepod on the camera display. The Captain answered in a matter-of-fact tone.

"ETs, coming to visit."

Alison spluttered in shock.

"Carl, pull up the recording of the ship."

"Aye, Cap'n."

Alison leaned closer to the display as the video from earlier came up on the screen.

"Holy shit," she breathed.

"That's what we thought," replied the Captain. "The main ship just detonated, and that lifepod is on intercept with us. What can we expect from these creatures?"

"How would I know?"

The Captain rested her hands on her hips and gave Alison a stern look.

"You're a doctor. A scientist. Make an educated guess."

Alison frowned in thought for a moment, then shook her head.

"It's hard to know where to start, with no data. Most of the more highly intelligent creatures we've catalogued are bipedal. They would almost certainly have opposable thumbs, if they are able to manufacture tools. Aside from that, who knows?"

The venting gasses in the video recording clicked in Carlton's mind.

"I may be able to help with that, hon. Just a sec."

He stilled the image again and selected the area around

the gas cloud, then keyed the spectrographic analyzer. Although the algorithm was optimized to analyze stellar composition and other natural phenomena, absorption and emission lines were the same everywhere. Maybe it could tell them what the venting gasses were.

Sure enough, after the computer chewed on the data for a minute or so, the spectral analysis popped up in a dialogue window.

"Ok, let's see. Looks like Oxygen and Nitrogen, with a fair amount of Helium and Carbon Dioxide."

"That could be engine fuel, or anything else, Carl."

"True, Cap'n, but it's better than nothing. If this is right, looks like about 25% Oxygen, 60% Nitrogen, 5% CO_2, 7% Helium, and the rest trace gasses."

Alison looked at the numbers and pursed her lips.

"That CO_2 concentration would be deadly for us to breathe. No telling if they could adjust to our lower concentration or not. Normal earth atmosphere would be like living at high altitude for them, but - "

" - we keep the O_2 levels lower than normal to reduce the chance of fires," Carlton finished for her. "What effect would breathing 17.5% O_2 have on them?"

"Probably the same as if we were to breathe 13%. Hypoxia."

"So Pericles is a deathtrap for them."

"Yes, but they don't know that," interjected the Captain. "Better to risk possible death than to accept it for certain. Alright, Carl, I'm going to need all hands for this. Sound Action Stations."

"Aye, Cap'n."

He pressed the first of a quartet of buttons on the starboard side of the pilot's station, and the pulsing tones of the ship's General Alarm sounded. Then the three of them made their way off the bridge.

CHAPTER THREE

S tandard procedure in the event of a general emergency was to muster the crew in the command center. By the time Carlton, Alison, and the Captain arrived, everyone else had gathered, the night shift looking mussed and bleary-eyed.

The Captain strode to the front of the small crowd with a brisk, business-like pace. Turning to face them, she placed her hands on her hips and spoke in a commanding tone.

"All right, people. We've got a situation. Carl, the video please."

Carlton stepped up to the main display screen's control workstation and tapped in a command.

The recording began playing on the screen, to a collective gasp from the crew. Their expressions ranged from awe to excitement to curiosity to fear as the Captain related the events leading up to Carlton sounding the General Alarm.

Malcolm, the Shift Engineer, spoke up in the silence that marked the conclusion of her briefing.

"How do we know it's a lifepod, and not a weapon of some kind?"

The Captain answered, "We don't. But it wouldn't make any sense to attack us, would it?"

"Fair enough. How long until it gets here?"

The Captain looked at Carlton, and he answered.

"It stopped accelerating and is running at .98c. It's 3.5 AU astern, so we have about fifteen and a half hours."

The Captain spoke again.

"We are obligated to render assistance, now that it is possible to do so without stranding ourselves. In the next fifteen hours, we need to figure out how we're going to do that, and then get it done."

There were protests, of course. Several of the crew wanted nothing to do with rescuing unknown aliens who may or may not have as their intention the slaughter of every human aboard so they could claim Pericles as their own. Only the inevitability of being overtaken whether they liked it or not got everyone onboard with the notion.

They set to work.

It was an easy decision to not bring the aliens aboard in section four, if only to keep them as far from the children as possible.

Section 2 contained hydroponics and consumables storage. There, it would be relatively easy, if time-consuming, for Malcolm and his techs to redirect some of the ventilation to raise the oxygen and carbon dioxide levels in a few compartments near the section 2 airlock, so the aliens would have a better chance at adjusting to the atmosphere. It would mean less carbon dioxide going to feed the crops, but in general they received more than they really needed, so it was a relatively safe move.

What to do with the aliens for the duration of the flight was another matter. Alison was hard-pressed to give an opinion as to whether the cryo-suspension units would be usable. They were designed to sustain humans, after all.

With no idea as to the aliens' metabolism, there was no telling what the units would do to them. All the same, she was able to modify a few unused units to supply gasses in closer proximity to the concentrations observed from the alien vessel.

That just left figuring out how to ask them to be guinea pigs. With all due respect to his wife and the Captain, Carlton wasn't about to place odds on their chances of accomplishing that.

The final question was how to get the aliens aboard. Carlton and Sven, his night-shift colleague, had that task. They brainstormed several ideas, but were unable to come up with a viable solution until Rachel, the teacher, reminded them of the mooring lights.

Pericles, like every starliner, had a number of moveable, high-powered spotlights mounted in various places on the hull. Their purpose was to aid in mooring, but the crews also put them to good use for other tasks. They were ready made to point the aliens where to go.

Early in the planning process, the Captain ruled out the airlocks in the crew's acceleration quarters or in the shuttle bay - Pericles had one short-range shuttle for commuting back and forth to space stations without full mooring facilities, stored in the same bay where the replacement nav beacons were housed. Getting the aliens from there to a suitable living area would be complex, and the crew would be in a less than optimal defensive posture, should things turn hostile.

That left the rings. Both were equipped with four airlocks, one in each section. Ring A's faced forward, Ring B's faced aft. The logical choice was the airlock to Section 2, Ring A.

Preparations took most of the time available, but the key players managed to swap a few hours of sleep before the rendezvous. With a half hour to go, the welcoming committee met in the command center.

The Captain, of course, would take the lead. Sven had relieved Carlton as pilot on duty, so Carlton had the job as the Captain's second. Alison would provide medical assistance, if needed. Malcolm insisted on coming along, with Bryce, Stephanie, and James, one of the horticulturists, in case things got ugly.

Carlton was surprised when the Captain agreed to that, and even more surprised when she ordered the small arms locker opened.

All starliners had a small cache of weapons onboard. Nothing special: a dozen slugthrowers and a few plasma rifles. Just enough for basic defense. The odds of ever needing to use them were very small, but there were a number of circumstances that might require it.

Carlton always viewed the weapons the same as a condom: better to have one and not need it, than to need one and not have it. All the same, except to conduct periodic inventories, he had never seen the small arms locker opened.

Carlton gave the Captain a wry grin as he strapped on a slugthrower. "Don't do anything provocative, right Cap'n?"

She sniffed. "Nothing in the procedure about committing suicide." Pulling the straps on her own holster tight, she straightened and looked over the other members of the team. "Everybody ready?"

They all nodded, doing their best to look calm. Bryce wasn't doing so well at acting, Carlton noticed. He licked his lips and adjusted his grip on his plasma rifle every few seconds, and his eyes darted around. He bore watching.

It took a few minutes to get to Section 2. Fortunately, each ring had an intra-ring transit system: a small railcar that allowed swift transport between the various sections. Without the rail, it would have been a long walk. Nevertheless, by the time they arrived at the airlock, there were only about ten minutes until the lifepod caught up with Pericles.

The airlock was a standard inner and outer door design. To the right of the inner door was a walk-in storage area containing spacesuits and emergency breathing equipment. On the other side, a display screen and control workstation was installed in the wall. Malcolm and Stephanie retrieved breathing equipment from the storage area while the Captain activated the workstation's intercom.

"All set at the airlock. How are our visitors?"

Sven answered promptly, from the command center.

"Five million kilometers astern and closing, Captain. Ready to secure ring rotation at your command."

"Is Janet ready?"

"Yes, ma'am."

"Right. Standby."

The Captain turned away from the console. She took a moment to don a breathing mask and tank, but didn't seal the mask, instead letting it hang loose around her neck.

Her poise impressed Carlton. He was about ready to jump out of his skin, anxious as he felt. But the Captain was in total control. He guessed that's why she got the big bucks.

"I'll order Janet to adjust atmospheres in this section after we're sure there's not going to be trouble. Be at the ready, but don't do anything to provoke them."

With that, she turned back to the workstation and keyed the ship-wide intercom.

"This is the Captain. We're about ten minutes from contact. Prepare for zero-G."

Her voice still echoed down the corridor as she switched back to the command center.

"Sven, secure ring rotation."

"Aye, Captain."

A pause followed while he keyed the command.

"Stopping sequence initiated. Band Brakes applied, thrusters firing. Rings will be secured in eight minutes."

"Very well."

The Captain tapped a few commands on the workstation, and the display screen came to life in two-pane format. The approaching lifepod appeared in one pane, and a high-level ship's status display appeared in the other. Already, the rings were beginning to slow perceptibly on the display. Carlton could feel a small force pushing him toward the far bulkhead as the ring slowed.

The Band Brakes were huge. Carlton had seen one of them removed from the ship's hub during the last maintenance upkeep. Even though he knew intellectually how large it had to be to slow the millions of kilograms of mass contained in each ring, he was nonetheless stunned when he saw it for himself. But large and powerful as they were, the Band Brakes were nowhere near enough to stop the rings all by themselves in any reasonable period of time, just as the Spinning Motors were not powerful enough to get the rings moving by themselves. So the starliners used thrusters, aligned to impart force in-line with or opposed to the rings' direction of rotation, to assist.

Over the next several minutes, the deceleration force remained small, but detectable. It wasn't enough to move an adult standing still, but if you were walking, you might find yourself turned without realizing it. Low mass loose objects and children tended to get pushed though, so procedure required checking all inhabited compartments for stowage and strapping the children in before starting or stopping the rings. More noticeable, the centripetal acceleration from the rings' movement lowered, making everything feel lighter.

Then there was no weight at all. The most minuscule movement pushed Carlton off the floor, and once more he found himself floating in zero-G. His favorite.

Sven's voice piped up over the intercom.

"Ring rotation secured, Captain. Zero-G in all compartments."

"Very well, Sven. Proceed as briefed. Let me know if anything unexpected occurs."

"Aye."

There was nothing to do but wait.

On the display screen, the range to the lifepod ticked down quickly, and its bearing rate began to increase. It looked like the aliens would pass down Pericles' port side. As the range lowered to ten thousand kilometers, the lifepod's forward velocity began lowering rapidly.

Interestingly, the blue-purple glow still appeared from that one location, near the far side of the craft. Carlton had presumed that glow was a thruster of some sort before. But if that were the case, it wouldn't be slowing them now, would it? It was puzzling.

The Captain shifted the other pane from ship's status to one of the hull monitoring cameras. Mounted astern the bridge, facing aft and upward, it provided a good view of the now-motionless rings and the section 2 airlock, stopped at the 2:30 position.

When the lifepod closed within a hundred kilometers, as briefed earlier, Sven shut off Pericles' hull illumination lights. Only the collision avoidance strobes, set at intervals around the rings, and the running lights at the bow and stern remained lit. In the hull monitoring camera, Pericles became a dim object, barely discernible from the interstellar darkness beyond. Then when the lifepod closed to 20 kilometers, Sven turned on four of the powerful spotlights. Two illuminated the lifepod itself, and two illuminated the Section 2 airlock outer door.

On the display, the lifepod image completely filled the aft upper camera's field of view, so the Captain shifted to a hull monitoring camera and tracked it in. Much harder to see without the large magnification, it took a couple minutes to find the lifepod as it stopped its relative motion amidships, about five kilometers to port. There it stayed for what seemed an eternity.

In reality, that eternity was just a few minutes. Carlton could imagine the conversation going on aboard the lifepod. "What do they intend?" "Should we go aboard or take our chances in the void?" "Foolish earthlings, don't they know we mean to kill them all and take their women?"

Well, on second thought the alien creatures would probably have no interest whatsoever in human women. But he couldn't rule out hostile intent in his mind, however dire the aliens' circumstances. He found himself reflexively fingering his slugthrower, and thinking maybe Bryce wasn't so far out of line in his jumpiness.

The lifepod turned and began to close Pericles. It quickly closed the kilometers from its holding position and took up position in front of the airlock.

The Captain shifted the camera view to one located not far from the airlock. From that angle, they could see the lifepod rotate in space until one of those circular markings Carlton saw earlier faced the airlock door. The lifepod began moving, ever so slowly, toward the airlock outer door, and everyone took a reflexive step backward.

Except the Captain. She remained at the workstation. As the lifepod drew near, she entered a command, and Carlton could see, through the windows on the inner door, the airlock outer door slide open. He swallowed, trying to loosen the lump in his throat. Glancing around, it looked as though his fellows were doing the same.

A tube extended from the lifepod.

A docking device, no doubt. But it was like no device Carlton had seen, because the end of the tube, where the sealing surface was, morphed in shape as it approached the airlock, until it exactly matched the mating surface on the outer airlock doorframe.

Carlton's jaw dropped as the lifepod made contact and the contact lights on the airlock status display illuminated. How did they do that?

He glanced at Malcolm, and saw he wasn't the only one surprised by this. It wasn't often that Malcolm was impressed, but he wore an awed expression on his face.

The Captain pressed a button on the workstation, and the display shifted to a camera inside the airlock. Carlton heard the hissing sound of rushing air, and the airlock interior pressure indication rose until it reached normal atmospheric, then held steady. One minute later, the pressure hadn't dropped. It was a good seal.

"Sven, positive seal on the airlock. Commence ring rotation."

Sven sounded more than a little on-edge when he responded.

"Aye, Captain. Spin sequence activated. Thrusters firing, Spinning Motors online."

Sven's voice came over the ship-wide intercom, announcing the imminent return of Gs. Then a moment later, ever so slowly, the ring started to move. The mating tunnel flexed a bit, but the seal held, and the lifepod began moving with the ring. The welcoming committee spread out as the closest bulkhead moved toward them. One by one, the team members struck it and pushed themselves down to the deck.

Carlton always found this part amusing. Ever so often, a newbie wouldn't watch himself when rotation started, and would end up getting tangled up with other people. This group was all seasoned, though, so the transition from zero-G to steadily building centripetal acceleration was smooth.

They re-arranged themselves in a semicircle around the

airlock inner door, with the Captain a pace ahead of the others. For a few minutes, nothing happened. The gravity slowly built, until they were at about two-thirds earth normal.

Then, on the display, Carlton saw the outer door on the lifepod slide open. This was it.

Four figures emerged from the lifepod. Dressed in loose-fitting grey garments that were not dissimilar to those the humans wore, the aliens were bipedal, as Alison predicted, but they had short tails. They walked barefoot, with a hunch, in quick, fluid steps.

Their gait changed abruptly as they passed from the mating tunnel into the airlock. A step that in the tunnel had barely made their heads bob caused their entire bodies to lift a centimeter or two off the deck.

"Artificial gravity," Malcolm said, echoing Carlton's thoughts. "How do they manage that without spinning, I wonder?"

The quartet paused in the airlock, and the humans got a better look at them on the display.

They were smaller than an average human, but appeared powerfully built. They wore breathing masks, but their facial features were clearly visible. They looked almost feline, with peaked ears atop their heads and elongated snouts. But they were hairless. Their skin was a yellow-orange color, with streaks of green, and it shimmered somewhat as they moved. It took Carlton a minute to figure out the reason: their skin was scaled. Their hands were three-fingered, with opposable thumbs - another point in Alison's favor. Their fingers ended in small points, rather than in pads.

The alien in front removed an instrument of some kind from a pouch on its belt. After studying the instrument for a moment, the alien made a gesture and said something. As it spoke, it revealed razor-sharp teeth and a green, flicking tongue.

All that was fine and dandy, but Carlton zeroed in on one last detail more than the others: they all had what looked like the hilt of a sword sticking up over their right shoulders, and what could only be holsters on their hips.

"Be ready," said the Captain, and she unsnapped the holster on her slugthrower. She noticed the weapons too.

From the corner of his eye, Carlton saw Bryce and Stephanie raise their plasma rifles to their shoulders. They all looked tense. Bryce was sweating up a storm.

The lead alien knocked on the inner door with the instrument it had just used. The sound traveled easily to Carlton's ears. For some reason, it seemed ominous.

"Alison, are you filming?"

Alison had refused the thought of carrying a weapon. She was a doctor, not an undertaker. Instead, she brought along a video recording device. Sven was making recordings of every external and internal camera feed, but few of them had audio, and they didn't cover every area that might be needed, so her recording was going to be the most vital.

"Yes."

"Alright. Malcolm, open the door."

Malcolm stood closest to the control station. He nodded and hit the inner door control switch.

The door opened. There was a slight hiss, and a small breeze, as the pressures between the two spaces equalized. The aliens stepped, one by one, into the room. They looked over the group of humans slowly, then the leader took a step toward the Captain.

"Oh Jesus," Bryce murmured, drawing Carlton's gaze. The guy was shaking badly. Malcolm, the closest to him, looked at Bryce with concern.

Either the Captain didn't hear or it didn't register. She managed a smile and said, "Welcome aboard."

The lead alien cocked its head to the side. It studied the

Captain for a moment after she spoke, then said something that sounded a mix between a hiss and a bark. The leftmost alien reached for its holster.

Bryce shouted, "OH JESUS!" and fired his plasma rifle.

Everything seemed to happen at once.

CHAPTER FOUR

The Captain screamed, "NO!"

The ball of superheated gas from Bryce's rifle struck the alien in the shoulder, sending it smashing into the bulkhead. It slumped to the ground, clutching at its wound.

The alien's neighbor bounded over to it and crouched down, to render assistance, no doubt.

The leader and the remaining alien turned to see their stricken comrade, for a heartbeat apparently as stunned as Carlton was.

Then they roared, their lips drawing back to reveal their teeth. Turning back to the humans, they seemed to coil as they dropped into low stances and advanced.

Malcolm tackled Bryce, bearing him to the floor and pinning him there. Bryce's rifle went skidding away out of his reach.

Stephanie stood there, a shocked expression on her face.

James fumbled at the snap on his holster.

Carlton found himself doing the same. Why wouldn't the cussed thing unsnap?

"NO!" shouted the Captain again. She jumped in front of the advancing creatures, her hands, empty, raised with palms facing them. "Stop!"

The lead alien grabbed the Captain by the throat and, with one hand, lifted her about twenty centimeters off the deck. It pulled its free hand back as though to punch, but Carlton saw what looked like razor-sharp claws unfolding from the points at the tips of its fingertips.

He got his holster unsnapped and drew his slugthrower. From the corner of his eye, he saw Stephanie sighting in on the leader.

"Don't shoot," the Captain managed to say, her voice sounding strangled.

She waved frantically at them with both hands, forceful downward gestures commanding them to lower their weapons.

Very reluctantly, Carlton complied, and he saw Stephanie do the same. James hadn't gotten his slugthrower out yet.

Malcolm pressed his forearm into the back of Bryce's neck and his knee into Bryce's kidney, drawing exclamations of pain from him.

The alien leader hissed, and its fellow stopped advancing.

The leader looked at the Captain for a long moment, then at Bryce and Malcolm, then at the others. Then, ever so slowly, it lowered the Captain to the ground.

With a bark, it released her and stepped back. The other alien stepped back as well, but its hand found the sword hilt, or whatever the thing was over its shoulder. The alien looked very ready to use it.

The Captain slumped backward, her hand going to her throat. She coughed heavily. Carlton moved forward to support her, but she brushed him aside.

"Alison," the Captain said, her voice still a bit strangled. "Help them."

Nodding, Alison passed the video recorder off to James, and, hefting her medical bag, moved toward the aliens.

She hadn't gone more than two steps before the alien with the sword stepped forward again, growling with menace. She swallowed and opened her bag. Withdrawing a roll of gauze, she held it up for the aliens to see.

The leader made another hiss-bark, in a different tone than the first, and the creature that was tending to their wounded comrade responded in kind.

The medic stood and helped its fellow to its feet. The wounded alien's shoulder was bound with narrow black bands of some material Carlton didn't recognize. It looked like they had first aid under control.

Alison nodded in understanding and backed up, replacing the gauze into her bag.

The leader made another bark, this time with a long, drawn-out hiss at the end. The alien medic led its wounded fellow through the airlock door. The patient gave the humans a look that, had a human made it, promised extreme violence. But it allowed itself to be led out without further incident.

When they left, the leader touched a button on the breast of its uniform. A soft beep sounded, and the leader began speaking, a quick succession of hisses, barks, growls, and whistles. A similar stream of alien words emanated from the button, clearly a communication device of some kind, in response. The leader bobbed its head and waited.

On the camera display, Carlton saw the lifepod's airlock door open again. Two new aliens stepped into the mating tunnel, pushing a large machine of some sort ahead of them.

The machine hovered in the air. Despite its obvious bulk, it appeared easy to maneuver down the tunnel and into Pericles' airlock. That hovering bit was a neat trick.

The leader moved aside as the new pair pushed the machine through the inner door and into the center of the room. The machine hovered half a meter above the floor, and was about two and a half meters long, a meter wide, and a meter and a half tall. Constructed of black metal, with a transparent hinged lid on top, it had a number of what looked like controls on one end. The lid was frosted over, making it difficult to see inside.

After they finished positioning the machine, the two new aliens turned and went back to the lifepod.

The leader stepped up to the machine and ran a hand over the lid. It was almost a caress.

The strangely tender moment ended quickly. The leader straightened and turned to the Captain. It made another sound, a cross between a hiss and a growl, and gestured for her to approach.

The Captain nodded and, swallowing, stepped forward. Carlton noticed she was being very careful to keep her hands empty and plainly in view. That didn't seem such a bad policy, considering.

The leader moved over to the machine's control panel and gestured again for the Captain to follow. When she reached its side, it pointed to a button on the panel and looked back at her. She nodded, and the leader touched the button. A low-frequency tone sounded, and the machine slowly lowered to the floor. The leader pressed the button again, and a higher frequency tone sounded. The machine rose from the floor and after a moment was hovering once more.

The leader lowered the machine back to the floor then moved to the next button. But before pushing it, the leader made a chopping motion with its free hand and issued another bark-hiss phrase. From the way it sounded out the words, whatever they were, Carlton surmised whatever the leader said was very important.

The leader pressed the second button, and the lid cracked

open. Clouds of steam poured through the crack. Carlton checked himself. That wasn't steam; it sank to the floor after it escaped the machine. It reminded him of melting dry ice.

The leader pushed the lid fully open and reached inside the machine. It withdrew an oval object, a bit larger than a baseball. It was green, streaked with yellow. It had a wrinkled, leathery texture, but appeared firm in the alien's grasp.

The leader turned back to the Captain and looked at her. Cradling the object in its arm, the leader gently pet it. Then, looking the Captain in the eyes, the leader pressed its free hand to its belly, then to the object.

"An egg," Alison said softly.

Stephanie gasped, and the Captain's eyes widened as the truth of Alison's analysis hit home.

The leader, apparently satisfied at their reactions, replaced the egg in the machine and pressed the second button. The lid shut with a solid click, and almost immediately frosted over again.

Turning back to the Captain, the leader then withdrew a rectangular black object from behind its belt. The object was about eight centimeters long, two and a half wide, and one centimeter deep. There were three raised red areas on it. The leader pointed to the first red area, and touched it.

In the space above the object, a three dimensional image appeared. The image was clearly holographic, an impressive enough feat that for a moment it distracted Carlton from what he was actually looking at: a star chart. In the lower portion of the image, a flashing green dot was visible, as well as a curved yellow line leading from the dot to a small star. Carlton knew his star charts well enough to recognize the green dot as their current location, and the small star as Sol. The aliens must have plotted out Pericles' course to determine their destination. It wouldn't be that hard to do.

The leader moved its finger into the image of Sol, and a new line, this one blue, appeared, leading from Sol across the chart to another, larger, star system. From what Carlton could tell of the scale, the second system was at least two hundred light years from Sol, well outside the area mankind had explored. The leader pointed at the Captain, then laid its hand on the machine. Finally, it pointed to the star system at the end of the blue line.

That couldn't mean what Carlton thought it meant, could it?

The Captain seemed to be having similar thoughts.

"Sir, we can't..."

The leader cut her off with a mixture growl and whistle. Then, again, it pointed from her to the machine to the star.

The Captain sighed and nodded.

The leader growled quickly, then pressed the second red area on the object.

The star chart disappeared, replaced by an image of the leader. It began speaking, more of the same grunts, growls, barks, and the rest. The speech cut off as the leader pressed the first red area again, and the star chart reappeared. It pointed at the second red area, then at the star at the end of the blue line.

The Captain nodded again, and the leader pressed the final red area.

One dot appeared, with a strange symbol next to it. A second later, that was replaced by two dots, with a different symbol. Then three, then four, all the way up to eight. Then different combinations of the symbols appeared, along with others. The image continued on like that for a minute or so, and then shifted to become a continuous sequence of symbols, probably a hundred fifty characters across and a hundred lines in length. The leader whistled, and waved its hand above the red area. The image shifted to another sequence, different from the first. Then, with another wave, yet another sequence appeared. What the hell was that supposed to be?

The Captain looked baffled also, but Malcolm's eyebrows had risen high onto his forehead. He wore an expression of awe. Catching Carlton's gaze, he spoke softly.

"It's their mathematics."

Carlton frowned. Why was that so impressive? Then it hit him. With knowledge of the aliens' mathematics, humans could translate scientific formulas, or technical specifications. Carlton would bet good money that's what those final pages of symbols were.

The leader pressed the third red area again, and the image disappeared. It pointed at the red area, then pointed at the Captain and the rest of the team in turn, even Bryce. Finally, with a low growl, followed by a bark, it held the rectangular object out toward the Captain.

Slowly, gingerly, she reached out and took it.

The leader made a hiss-bark similar to one it made earlier, and its companion backed away into the airlock. When it had gone, the leader made a strangely intricate gesture with its hands, ending with an inclination of its head toward the Captain. Then, it turned and strode out of the room, into the airlock.

"Where's he going?" Carlton asked.

The entire welcoming committee moved to the inner airlock door, all save Bryce, who remained lying on the floor, despite Malcolm releasing him from the submission hold.

The alien leader didn't look back, but walked straight into the lifepod's airlock. The door shut quickly behind it.

They all looked at each other in confusion, and no small amount of shock. Then lights began flashing in the mating tunnel, and a oscillating siren sounded. Malcolm's eyes widened, and he quickly moved to the airlock control console. He hit a button, and the outer airlock doors slid shut.

No sooner had they done so than the mating tunnel detached. Through the small window in the outer airlock doors, they saw the tunnel begin to retract, then it and the lifepod disappeared, leaving nothing visible but the slowly rotating starfield.

The Captain rushed to the workstation and called up the external camera view. Nothing. She hit the intercom to the command center.

"Sven! Where did it go?"

Sven, sounding nearly breathless, responded promptly.

"Just off the starboard side, Captain, moving away at about seventy meters per second. Wait. Velocity is increasing rapidly. Gained visual on the number 6 hull monitoring camera."

"Right." She called up that camera, and they all saw the lifepod moving quickly away. Very soon it was too far away to make out without additional magnification, and she shifted to the forward upper camera, which Sven directed to track the lifepod.

Malcolm hit the control for the inner door, and it slid shut. Then he spoke.

"It makes sense, Captain. They would have continued on in the same direction as the velocity vector they had the instant before they detached. On the first deck, the rings rotate at about seventy meters per second, so..."

The Captain interrupted him.

"I understand physics, Malcolm. Why the hell did they leave?"

Bryce, still lying there with his face pressed to the floor, sobbed.

"I'm sorry, Captain. I was so scared. I thought it was pulling a gun."

The Captain gave him a withering look. Good thing for him he couldn't see it, or he'd either turn to stone or burst into flame. Then her expression softened. Carlton was surprised by that, but not by her reply.

"It's alright, Bryce. We were all scared. I shouldn't have put you in that position."

Bryce looked up, a grateful expression on his face. Then, wiping his nose, he sat up. Probably he didn't get the deeper meaning to her statement. Carlton was sure Bryce would never see high-stress tasking again. He did not know it, but his career just came to a standstill, at least on this ship.

Carlton cleared his throat.

"Am I crazy, or did they just ask us to..."

He stopped speaking as a bright flash on the display drew his, and everyone else's, attention. His eyes went wide as he realized what he was seeing. Where the lifepod used to be, there was only an expanding cloud of hot gasses and shrapnel.

The Captain hit the intercom again.

"Sven! How far was it when it blew?"

"Five hundred kilometers, Captain. I'm tracking the largest fragments. They should pass well clear of us."

The Captain let out a breath, her expression one of relief.

"Very well."

She switched to the ship-wide intercom.

"Attention, this is the Captain. Our visitors have departed. Resume normal watch routine. That is all."

With that, she turned back to the group. Nodding to Carlton, she spoke again.

"Yes, Carl, they did. They want us to deliver their eggs to their homeworld."

From her tone of voice, she was just as confused as he felt. Malcolm spoke up.

"Probably that reading they took in the airlock is what did it, Captain." He held up a hand to forestall a retort. "They got data on our atmosphere as soon as they entered the tunnel. When they got to the airlock, they also got data on our gravitation. They probably realized they couldn't survive on our ship for long, and went with plan B. The eggs are on ice. Don't need the same resources they do. So at least they have a chance to preserve something of themselves. Assuming we keep our end of the deal."

"Why should we?" James asked. "We've got enough to worry about."

"They paid us, for one thing," Malcolm retorted.

"And it's the right thing to do," the Captain added. She looked at the alien machine, with its precious cargo, and sighed. "Let's get this thing stowed. Malcolm, figure out what kind of power it needs and rig up something to provide it."

Malcolm looked askance at her and opened his mouth to reply, but stopped after a second and nodded, saying nothing.

The Captain traced her fingers along the length of the artifact and pursed her lips. "Carl, we're going to have one hell of a message to send. Get a draft ready for review by the end of this watch. For the rest of you," she looked at each crewmember in turn, "as far as anyone off this ship knows, this never happened. No talking about it except for what is necessary for shift turnover."

"You're not really thinking of changing course?" James sounded incredulous, but also afraid.

The Captain shook her head, shooting him a withering look. "Of course not. We don't have the fuel for that sort of adjustment. And besides, we've got passengers and cargo who need to get to Earth. When we get there, we'll turn this thing over to the authorities, and they will see it sent home."

"So much for the boring center passage," Carlton said, trying to insert a bit of humor.

The Captain looked at him, but her expression was one of resignation. She shook her head and sighed again. "Space travel sucks sometimes, doesn't it?"

PREVIEW OF THE PERICLES CONSPIRACY

First Contact is complete, but the story is far from over. The adventure continues in The Pericles Conspiracy, a science fiction thriller from Michael Kingswood and SSN Storytelling.

CAPTAIN JOSEPHINE ISHIKAWA changed the course of history, but no one knows about it.

She and her crew had an encounter while returning to Earth from the colony worlds, and upon their arrival the government swore them to secrecy about it.

With the powers that be in charge, Jo did her best to put the incident out of her mind and set about getting her starliner, Pericles, through a major overhaul and back out to the stars.

But the circumstances of their return to Earth along with the mysterious death of her Chief Engineer has caused the news media to ask questions, prompting Jo to wonder whatever became of the beings she rescued out in the depths of space, and of the promise she made to their dying parents.

If you like action and intrigue, The Pericles Conspiracy is sure to keep you on the edge of your seat, and leave you wanting more.

PICK-UP LINES

L a Chupacabra was almost empty.

A few patrons sat at tables along the wall opposite the bar and two more were at the bar itself: a plump middle-aged man in dirty work coveralls at the near corner and, at the far end, a slender woman with short-cut black hair dressed in dark business attire.

The bartender idly wiped down the taps halfway down the bar, and a lone waitress chatted with a patron at one of the tables.

Vidscreens behind the bar displayed the latest headlines and sports scores, but the volume was muted. A tune from the middle of the pop charts played over the bar's speakers, just loudly enough to make it difficult to hear a conversation from more than a few feet away.

He would have expected more business, considering it was hump day. Just two more days until the weekend after all. But he was just as happy for a sparse crowd. He hated having to search through a throng to find his mark.

As it was, a quick survey as he paused at the tavern's

entrance revealed this evening's objective. He smiled slightly and walked to the far end of the bar.

He paused as he reached the chair around the corner of the bar from the slender woman. He cleared his throat, but the woman already noted his presence, favoring him with a slight frown and a quirked eyebrow.

"Is this seat taken?" he asked.

She shrugged and looked away, back to the closest vidscreen, where, from what he could tell from the closed-captioning, some talking head was pontificating about what effect the latest elections on Centauri would have on inter-stellar trade.

Her choice of programming made sense, considering her occupation.

As he sat down, he was struck by the woman's appearance. Ten year-long shifts as Captain on a starliner, plus the time to move up through the ranks to reach that station meant she had to be in her early to mid 50s at least. Still, he could have sworn she still had a few decades before she reached her middle years: she did not look a day over forty.

Her bio said she was the product of a marriage between a Japanese man and an English woman. In his experience, women from east Asia tended to age well, but even still he was impressed.

The bartender sauntered over.

"What'll it be?"

"Bud Light."

He noticed the woman smirk ever so slightly before taking a sip of her drink as the bartender moved back to the taps. He figured she would prefer to drink something more exotic from one of the colony worlds, but unless he missed his guess, she was drinking a Seven and Seven.

Hardly the height of sophistication itself, and not exactly a perch from which to scoff at his beer.

"You ever study ancient history?"

She glanced back at him and rolled her eyes.

"I'm not looking for company right now."

"Sorry. Don't mean to impose."

She sniffed and turned back to her newsvid.

A moment later the bartender returned with his beer. He accepted it with a smile of thanks and tapped the paypad on the bar. His database implant interfaced with the pay system and applied his standard tip rate automatically. The bartender looked surprised, then pleased, and voiced his thanks before moving away.

Tipping well was often useful for opening doors, he found.

He sipped at his beer for a few minutes, watching the newsvid with only the vaguest of interest. It was a moot discussion; whatever effects the election caused had already occurred more than four years ago. Folks on Earth were only now hearing about it, of course. But whatever changes they made in response would also be extremely time late in reaching Centauri ears.

So what was the point?

Glancing back at the woman, he noted that she too looked a bit amused at the discussion. Of course, she would know the futility of it more than most.

Time to try again.

"So I was reading the other day about an ancient Athenian ruler. Guy named Pericles."

She stiffened slightly when he mentioned the name, but quickly recovered, sipping her drink again without bothering to look at him.

"Is that right?" She sounded annoyed.

"Very interesting man." He took another drink of his beer. "He took over while Athens was rebuilding from the Persian wars. He fostered the arts, built the Acropolis, endorsed Athenian expansionism. During his reign, Athens became the greatest political force in the region. But then, of course, he pressed too far. Made Sparta nervous. And so, the Peloponnesian War. He didn't live to see it, but eventually Athens fell beneath Sparta's military might."

"Fascinating. Look, I *really* don't want company, so..."

"I heard a story about another Pericles recently."

She froze, her expression suddenly becoming wary. He continued on.

"Starliner by that name comes in from the Gliese system, just like normal. But there's nearly a week's delay in unloading the cargo. The crew is sequestered. Interviewed by government agents, they say. All but the fourth shift are out within a week. That shift's sequestered for more than a month. Six months later, Malcolm Ngubwe, the fourth shift's Engineer, dies under, shall we say, mysterious circumstances? Then that same shift's pilot, one Carlton Hersch, and his wife Alison, the shift's doctor, leave the starliner company for work planetside." He shrugged. "Not so unusual, except he was in line for promotion to Captain. Strange time for a career change, isn't it?"

"I don't know what you're talking about."

"Yes you do." He leaned toward her, noting her expression shifting from wariness to nervousness. "What happened out there to cause so much fuss, Captain Ishikawa?"

She swallowed, pulling away from him.

"Who are you?"

He tapped his thumb and forefinger and waited for a moment.

When nothing happened, he sniffed in annoyance. He figured she would have upgraded to the interactive database implant by now. She had been back long enough, and those implants made forgetting names a thing of the past.

He always kept old-style holocards, though, just in case.

Pulling one from his pocket, he slid it across the bar to

her. His credentials were plainly visible: Jeremy Reynolds, Investigative Reporter, Star News.

She picked it up, her eyes narrowing as she read it. Then she stood, dropping the card onto the bar.

"I've got nothing to say to you, Mr. Reynolds."

She turned to leave, but stopped as Jeremy grabbed her arm gently.

"There are rumors of a new strain of disease onboard. The public has a right to know the truth, Captain."

She hesitated, then pulled away from his grasp.

"Good night, Mr. Reynolds."

With that, she walked away at a brisk pace. She was out the door quickly, and never looked back.

Jeremy remained in his chair for several minutes more, finishing his beer and shrugging off the bartender's quip about him striking out. There was definitely something there. And he intended to find out what it was.

THE PERICLES CONSPIRACY is available now for purchase in all online bookstores. Buy your copy today!

MESSAGE FROM THE AUTHOR

Thank you for reading my book. I hope you enjoyed reading it as much as I enjoyed writing it.

Every review helps an author out, so whether you loved this book, hated it, or something in between, please take a minute to tell other readers what you thought. All of the online retailers make it very easy to do, and I would really appreciate it.

Feel free to come say hi at my website or on Facebook. I always enjoy hearing from readers, especially since you all are, collectively, my boss.

I also have a weekly podcast, Story Time With Michael Kingswood, where I read stories and talk through some of the latest goings on in my world. I'd love to see you there.

Thanks again. My best to you and yours.

Warm Regards,
Michael Kingswood

MAILING LIST

If you enjoyed this book and would like word on new releases and special deals from Michael Kingswood, sign up for his newsletter on his website. Guaranteed to be spam-free, you can opt out at any time. And you can rest assured he will not share your information with anyone, for any reason.

https://michaelkingswood.com/newsletter-signup/

SUPPORTING PATRONAGE

Michael would like to invite you to become a supporting member of his website. Similar in concept to Patreon, a few dollars a month will give you access to exclusive content, and help him to focus more of his time to writing fun and exciting stories for your enjoyment.

Sign up at his website:

https://www.michaelkingswood.com/membership/supporting-patronage/

ABOUT THE AUTHOR

Michael Kingswood is 20-year veteran of the US Navy submarine force and a lifelong fan of science fiction and fantasy literature. His work has appeared in numerous collections and anthologies, to include the Fiction River Anthology series from WMG publishing. He holds a bachelors degree in Mechanical Engineering as well as a Master of Engineering Management and a Master of Business Administration. He has four children and currently resides in San Diego.

Find Michael Kingswood online at:

www.michaelkingswood.com

www.facebook.com/michael.kingswood

steemit.com/@michaelkingswood

MORE BOOKS BY MICHAEL KINGSWOOD

GLIMMER VALE CHRONICLES

Glimmer Vale

Out-Dweller

Tollard's Peak

Robbed Blind

Wedding Gifts: A Glimmer Vale Chronicles Story

The Falconer's Stairs

Glimmer Vale Omnibus Edition #1

THE PERICLES CONSPIRACY

Passing In The Night

The Pericles Conspiracy

DAWN OF ENLIGHTENMENT

Masters Of The Sun

NOVELLAS

What Lurks Between

The Necromancer's Lair

The Champion

Veritas Morte

STORY COLLECTIONS

Tales Of Adventure #1

Tales Of Adventure #2

Short Story 10-Pack

A Jar Of Mixed Treats

SHORT FICTION

Michael has also published a number of shorter works, links to
which can be found on his website.